Wolf Pie

Wolf Pie

by Brenda Seabrooke

Illustrated by Liz Callen

Clarion Books
Houghton Mifflin Harcourt
New York • Boston

Clarion Books
215 Park Avenue South, New York, New York 10003
Text copyright © 2010 by Brenda Seabrooke
Illustrations copyright © 2010 by Liz Callen

The illustrations were executed in pencil, watercolors, and digital media.
The text was set in 14-point Cooper.

Clarion Books is an imprint of Houghton Mifflin Harcourt Publishing Company.

www.hmhbooks.com

Printed in Singapore

Library of Congress Cataloging-in-Publication Data

Seabrooke, Brenda.
Wolf pie / by Brenda Seabrooke ; illustrated by Liz Callen.
p. cm.
Summary: When Wilfong the wolf fails to blow down the house of
the Pygg brothers, he stays outside their door all winter learning their games
and listening to their jokes and stories, but although he claims to be reformed,
the pigs are reluctant to offer friendship.

ISBN 978-0-547-04403-3

[1. Wolves—Fiction. 2. Pigs—Fiction. 3. Friendship—Fiction.]
I. Callen, Liz, ill. II. Title.

PZ7.S4376Wol 2010
[E]—dc22

2009015820

TWP 10 9 8 7 6 5 4 3 2 1

4500208448

To Ian and his cousins
Alex, Nick, and Audrianna
—B.S.

To Burt and Belinda.
At last! Pigs really do fly . . .
—L.C.

1

Clonk! Clonk! Clonk!

James Pygg and his brothers were building a new house on Buttercup Lane.

"Bricks are heavy," whined Marvin. "Why can't we use something light—like sticks?"

"Or hay," whined Lester, "so it won't take so long."

"We need a strong, sturdy house, so we'll be safe in winter," said James. "That's when food is scarce and wolves come looking for pigs to eat." He slapped another brick on the wall.

Marvin and Lester shivered. They were afraid of hungry wolves. They stopped complaining and worked hard.

By the end of the summer, the house was finished. The Pyggs stocked it with plenty of food and moved in. James locked the doors. His brothers latched the tight-fitting windows.

"Now we're safe and snug," James said.

Just as they sat down to supper, someone banged the knocker on the front door. *Clonk! Clonk! Clonk!*

"Open up!" demanded a scary voice.

The Pyggs peeked through the front window.

"It's a wolf!" squealed Marvin.

"He's going to eat us!" screamed Lester.

They crawled under the table.

"Don't worry," said James. "He can't get in."

The knocker banged again. *Clonk! Clonk! Clonk!*

"You're early, Mr. Wolf. You're not supposed to be here till winter," James called loudly. "And please stop that knocking. You're giving me a headache."

"I'll be glad to stop," said the wolf, "*if* you open the door."

"Don't be silly," said James. "We built our house strong and sturdy to keep you out."

The wolf flew into a rage. "If you won't let me in, I'll blow your house down!" he snarled. He huffed and puffed. He puffed and huffed. The house didn't budge.

Neither did the wolf.

"If you won't let me in, I won't let you out," he said, and he sat down by the door.

Days passed. Autumn leaves fell, and a chilly wind began to blow. *Whoosh! Whooosh! Whoooosh!* The wolf was cold and hungry, but he wouldn't give up, and he wouldn't go away. He watched the Pyggs through the window.

"Lester's behind the blue chair!" he yelled when they played hide-and-seek.

"Marvin has two kings," he announced when they played cards.

And when they played riddle-me-this, he wanted to guess, too.

"Here's one," said James. "What's black and white and red all over?"

"I know! I know!" the wolf called, jumping up and down and waving his paw.

"It's tracks in the snow at sunset," said Marvin.

"No," said Lester, "it's—"

"A newspaper!" interrupted the wolf. "Black print on white paper that's *read* all over!"

"That's what *I* was going to say, smarty wolf," said Lester.

"Wilfong," said the wolf. "My name is Wilfong."

One evening, James read a story out loud. The wolf listened, too. "What happened after that?" he asked as James closed the book.

"That's the end of the story," said James.

"But I want to know what happened in happily ever after," said the wolf. "Did Cinderella break her glass slippers? Were the mice different after they'd been horses? What happened to the pumpkin coach?"

"Good questions," said James. "I think Cinderella put her slippers in a display case in the castle. The mice went back to squeaking, but once in a while they let out an embarrassing neigh. And the pumpkin was made into a giant pie and served at Cinderella's wedding."

"I like that ending," said the wolf.

"It does tie up all the loose ends," James agreed.

When the Pyggs sang around the piano, the wolf howled along with them. *"Awoo, awoo, awooooo!"* He was almost on key.

When winter arrived, the Pygg brothers made hot chocolate. "Maybe the wolf would like some," said Lester. Marvin filled a mug, and James put it on the windowsill.

"Thanks," said the wolf. He slurped his steaming chocolate.

When the first snowflakes began to fall, the Pygg brothers felt sorry for the wolf. They put pizza and popcorn and slices of yum-yum cake on the windowsill for him.

The wolf gobbled them up. *"Yum, yum, yum!"* Pig food tasted much better than pigs.

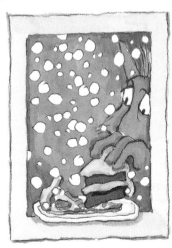

As snow piled up around him, the wolf's teeth chattered with cold. *Clickety-click! Clickety-clack!*

"P-p-p-please, g-g-guys, let me c-c-come in," he begged.

"No," said James. "You're a wolf."

"Wilfong. My n-n-name is W-w-wilfong," said the wolf as he shivered and shook. Soon he turned blue. His teeth stopped chattering, and he didn't move.

"I think he's frozen," said Marvin.

"What can we do?" asked Lester.

"Let's try to warm him up," said James.

Marvin tugged mittens onto the wolf's paws. Lester tied a hat on his head. James wrapped a long woolly scarf around his neck. They put a blanket over his back. But the wolf stayed frozen all winter long.

In spring, a flower popped up. It tickled the wolf's nose, and he sneezed. *Achoo! Achoo! Achoo!* Chunks of ice fell off his nose, his tail, and his back. *Plink, plank, plunk.*

The Pygg brothers ran outside. They were glad the wolf had defrosted. They weren't afraid of him now. It was warm. The woods and fields were full of green and growing things. There was plenty of food for everyone.

"You can go home now, wolf," said James.

"Shoo, wolf," said Marvin.

"Scram, wolf," said Lester.

"Wilfong, my name is Wilfong," said the wolf. "And I don't want to go. Can't I live with you?"

"No," said James. "You're still a wolf."

"But I like it here," said Wilfong. "I learned to sing. I like your games and riddles and stories. I don't want to eat pigs anymore. Your food is better.

Please let me live with you. I'll be a good wolf, I promise. I'm reformed."

The Pyggs looked at each other. "All right," said James. "We'll give you a chance. I have a plan."

The Pygg brothers and Wilfong built a little wolf room onto the side of the sturdy brick house. The room had a door, but it only led outside. The window between the house and the wolf room had a latch on the Pyggs' side. They could open the window to pass pizza and popcorn and slices of yum-yum cake *out*, but Wilfong couldn't get *in*.

He was reformed, but he was still a wolf.

From then on, Wilfong sat at his window every evening. He listened to the stories James read out loud. He traded riddles with the Pyggs. But when they played hide-and-seek, they made him wear a blindfold so he couldn't tell where everyone was hiding.

Wilfong didn't mind. He was having fun. "*Awoo, awoo, awooooo!*" he sang along with the Pygg brothers. He was almost on key.

2
Urp! Urp! Urp!

One summer day, the Pygg brothers were working in their garden. Wilfong watched from his window.

"I'm hot," whined Marvin.

"Me, too," whined Lester. "Can't we stop now?"

"Not yet," said James. "We have to finish weeding if we want vegetables this winter."

"Who wants vegetables?" said Marvin. "We only want pizza."

"And popcorn," said Lester.

"Don't forget yum-yum cake," said Wilfong.

"There's your popcorn," James said, pointing to a row of tall cornstalks. "And over there are the tomatoes and peppers for pizza, and all the vegetables we put in soup."

"Where's the yum-yum cake growing?" asked Wilfong.

"We have to make that from ingredients we buy at the store," said James. "We trade the storekeeper vegetables for the things we need. So if you want cake, pull those weeds."

Marvin and Lester put their heads down and weeded.

When they'd all finished their rows, James stood up. He checked the garden. There wasn't a weed in sight. "Now we can play," he said. "Let's go to the beach."

"Yay!" said Marvin.

"Yay!" said Lester.

"Me, too?" asked Wilfong.

The Pygg brothers looked at each other. Wilfong didn't scare them anymore, but he was still a wolf. They had to be careful.

"All right," said James, "if you promise to behave."

"I'll behave," said Wilfong. "I'm reformed— remember?"

On the bus ride to the beach, the three brothers sat together. Wilfong sat by himself. He leaned over the back of his seat to talk to the Pyggs. Riding backward made him bus-sick, and he had to urp out the window. *Urp! Urp! Urp!*

The Pygg brothers shared a room at the hotel. Wilfong had to bunk alone across the hall. They all put on swimsuits, raced to the beach, and jumped into the ocean together.

They were having a great time until a wave knocked Wilfong over. The Pygg brothers had to help him up and take him back to shore.

They built a castle. Wilfong got sand in his fur, and it made him itch. His nose turned red from sunburn, and it was so sore, he cried. His salty tears made his nose sting worse.

James put cream on Wilfong's sunburn. He gave him a hat and sunglasses to wear. Marvin and Lester brushed his fur clean.

That night they all went to the boardwalk.

The Pygg brothers rode the Ferris wheel together. Wilfong rode alone. He was scared and got Ferris-wheel-sick. He had to get off to urp. Then they all rode the roller coaster. *Everybody* was scared, but only Wilfong urped.

Wilfong liked the bumper cars and the merry-go-round. Everybody rode alone on those, and nobody got sick. Not even Wilfong.

The Pygg brothers were having fun.

"I'm having fun, too," said Wilfong. He tried to grin, but it was a wobbly wolf grin.

The Pygg brothers felt sorry for him. James shared his cotton candy. Marvin shared his candy apple. Lester shared his candy popcorn. Wilfong felt better for a little while. Then he turned green and urped into a trash can. *Urp! Urp! Urp!*

The Pygg brothers took him to his room and tucked him into bed. They went back to the board-walk. Wilfong was a wobbly green wolf, alone in his room.

The next morning, James made Wilfong stay in bed while he and his brothers went to the beach. Wilfong felt sorry for himself all alone in his room, but by afternoon, he was wolf-colored again.

"All that rest made you well," said James. "You can come to the beach with us, but you should stay in the shade."

The Pyggs rented a beach umbrella for Wilfong, and they all sat under it to play cards. Wilfong felt sleepy. He stretched out on a towel and went to sleep. Zzz . . . Zzzzz . . . Zzzzzz . . .

The Pygg brothers blew up their raft. They climbed aboard and floated on the wide blue sea. Waves bumped against the raft. *Slish, slosh, slush.*

The soft sounds lulled the Pyggs to sleep. While they snoozed, a riptide pulled their raft out to sea. When they woke up, they were far from the shore.

"Help!" called Marvin

"Help!" yelled Lester.

"Paddle!" shouted James.

The Pygg brothers paddled hard, but the riptide was too strong. It pulled the raft farther out to sea.

Wilfong woke up. Where were James and Marvin and Lester? He shaded his eyes and looked around. The raft was a tiny dot on the wide blue sea, but he could see the Pyggs onboard. They were waving for help.

He leaped up. He didn't feel wobbly now. He felt strong—as strong as a wolf. The Pygg brothers needed to be rescued. But who would help him do it? The beach was empty. He would have to save them by himself. But how? James always had a plan. Now Wilfong needed one.

He spied a sailboat pulled up on shore. Suddenly, he knew what to do! He dragged the boat into the water and jumped onboard. The boat didn't move. The sail hung as limp as a curtain.

Wilfong licked his paw and held it up to test the breeze. There wasn't one—but that was no problem. Wilfong was a wolf, after all. He sucked in a deep gulp of air. Then he puffed out a giant wolf breath.

The sail billowed and filled. The boat skimmed across the waves. *Skip, skap, skeee.*

Wilfong huffed and puffed. The boat sailed faster. Wilfong puffed and huffed. The boat zoomed over the sea.

Soon the Pyggs spied their rescuer. "It's Wilfong!" they all shouted. "Hooray!"

When the sailboat reached the raft, the Pygg brothers scrambled aboard. James tied the raft behind, and Wilfong turned the boat around. He huffed and puffed it back to shore.

Now the beach was crowded with people. They had watched Wilfong rescue the three Pyggs, and they raised a cheer as he brought the boat to shore. *"Yay! Yaay! Yaaaaay!"*

Wilfong was a hero. He posed with the Pyggs for pictures.

"Thank you, Wilfong," said James. "You saved us with your wolf breath."

"You're a good wolf," said Marvin.

"The best," said Lester.

"You're our friend," said James.

The three brothers took Wilfong to the boardwalk. They rode all the rides together. Wilfong wasn't scared, and he didn't turn green. He didn't urp a single time!

That night Wilfong bunked with the Pyggs. And when they went home the next day, he didn't get bus-sick. He sat with his friends and smiled all the way back to Buttercup Lane.

3

Yum! Yum! Yum!

One morning, James Pygg opened his front door. The newspaper lay by the step, but he didn't pick it up. Instead, he slammed the door and locked it.

"Wolves!" he whispered to his brothers. "All around our house!"

Marvin and Lester peeped out the window.

"Help!" screamed Marvin. "Those wolves have come for dinner!"

"And we're the dinner!" screamed Lester. "Help! Help! Help!"

"Nonsense," said James. "We're safe in our sturdy brick house. Those wolves can't get in."

"But we can't go out," cried Marvin. "Ever!"

"We'll starve!" whimpered Lester. "And *then* they'll eat us!"

"No, they won't," said James. "Wilfong will make them go away."

Marvin and Lester were not so sure. Wilfong was

their friend, but he was a wolf, too. They hid behind the sofa.

James knocked on the window of Wilfong's room. "We're surrounded by wolves," he said. "Tell them to go away, please."

Wilfong looked out his door. Big wolves. Little wolves. Tall wolves. Short wolves. Wolves of all sizes and shapes lolled around the house.

"Er . . . I'll talk to them," said Wilfong. But he wasn't at all sure they would listen. The wolves looked hungry. And there's nothing more stubborn than a hungry wolf—except a pack of hungry wolves.

Wilfong went outside. "Morning," he said to the wolves.

The head wolf came right to the point. "We heard you live in a house with pigs," he said. "Is that true?"

"Well, sort of," Wilfong said. "I live in a room that's *attached* to a house with pigs."

A wolf cheer rang out. *"Yum! Yum! Yum!"*

Marvin and Lester shook with fright. James felt sick.

"How should we cook 'em?" asked a plump wolf.

"How many have you got?" asked the head wolf.

"Er . . . enough," said Wilfong. "But I don't think we should cook them."

"You like 'em raw?" asked the plump wolf. "Me, I like 'em baked with cloves and brown sugar."

"Yes. I mean no. I mean, I like them the way they are," said Wilfong. "The Pyggs are my friends."

"Friends!" screamed the head wolf.

"Friends!" screamed the rest of the pack.

"Yes," said Wilfong. "I don't eat pigs anymore."

The head wolf grabbed Wilfong by his shirt front. "Listen," he said. "You're giving wolves a bad name. More important, we're hungry and we came here to eat. So if we don't have pig for dinner, we'll have to have *you*. Understand?"

Wilfong gulped. "I understand," he said.

"Then hurry up," said the head wolf.

"Yeah," said the others. "We're really hungry." And they began to drool.

"He's going to cook us, and the wolves are going to eat us!" cried Marvin.

"I'm scared," said Lester. "Will it be dark inside a wolf?"

"You won't know," said Marvin. "You'll be all chewed up."

"So will you," said Lester.

Marvin and Lester both fainted. Even James turned pale. But he trusted Wilfong. So when his friend knocked on the window between the wolf

room and the house, he opened it wide enough for Wilfong to climb through.

"What are we going to do?" Wilfong whispered to James. "That's a bunch of big bad wolves out there."

"If we feed them, they'll go away," said James.

"But they want to eat pig!" said Wilfong.

"Then we'll just have to give it to them," said James. "I have a plan."

Marvin and Lester sat up.

"What is it?" asked Wilfong.

"We'll make pig pot pie for them," said James.

"Where will we get the pigs?" Wilfong asked.

Marvin and Lester got ready to faint again.

"We won't," said James. "We'll only *tell* them it's pig pot pie. They won't know it's not."

"Those wolves have been around," said Wilfong. "They know pig pot pie."

"We'll fool them," said James. "You'll see. Here's what we'll do." And he told them his plan.

Marvin and Lester didn't faint. They grinned sneaky pig grins. Wilfong grinned a wolfish grin.

Wilfong got a cleaver from the kitchen drawer.

He stood near the window where the wolves could see him. Then he raised the cleaver—and brought it down with a loud *whomp* on a pillow. The Pygg brothers sat out of sight and squealed as loudly as they could. Wilfong raised the cleaver again. *Whomp! Whomp! Whomp!*

One by one, the Pygg brothers fell silent. James was last. He broke off in mid-squeal.

Outside, the wolves heard the squeals stop. The drool dripped off their chins.

Wilfong rolled out dough for the pot pie crusts. Then he got out the cutting board and began to mince and chop. *Chop! Chop! Chop!* He sang a wolf song while he worked. *"Awoo, awoo, awooooo!"* He filled the oven with pies.

The wolves smelled them cooking. "Yum!" they said. They smacked their lips. They slobbered and drooled all over their clothes.

When the pot pies came out of the oven, Wilfong wheeled them outside on a tea cart.

The wolves didn't even wait for them to cool. They grabbed the hot pies and fell to eating. They had no manners at all. They grunted and smacked. They chomped and slobbered. They gulped and slurped. They ate like a pack of wolves. Then they lay around the yard with their stomachs sticking up like little wolf hills.

"That was good pig pot pie," said the head wolf. "The best I've ever eaten."

The other wolves nodded. Some of them burped. *Burrup. Barrup. Bourrup.* Others belched. *Belch. Beeelch. Beeeelch.* They made a lot of noise.

"I'm glad you liked it," said Wilfong. "But it wasn't pig pie. It was wolf pie."

"Wolf pie!" screamed the head wolf.

"Wolf pie!" screamed the other wolves.

"Wolf pie," said Wilfong. "The best I've ever made."

The wolves fainted in a giant pile of fur in the middle of the yard.

"*Tsk, tsk, tsk,*" said Wilfong. "Where are all the big bad wolves now?" He turned on the outside water tap and hosed off the whole pack.

The wolves came to and staggered around. They shook their dripping heads. They flung droplets from their fur. They wrung water from their sopping tails.

"Are you done fainting?" Wilfong asked.

"I think so," gasped the head wolf. "Who's missing?"

The wolves counted off. Everybody was there.

"Who did you cook?" asked the head wolf.

"Nobody," said Wilfong. "Those weren't real wolf pies. They were fake wolf pies. I made them with beans and carrots and peas and potatoes."

"Vegetables?" screamed the head wolf in horror.

"Vegetables?" screamed the other wolves.

"Is there an echo here?" asked Wilfong. "Yes, those were vegetable pot pies. No pig. No wolf."

"But we heard pigs squealing," said the head wolf.

"That was part of the plan," Wilfong said. "We tricked you, the Pyggs and I." He grinned wolfishly.

The Pygg brothers waved through the window at the wolves.

The wolves grinned sheepishly. They had been tricked, but now they were hungry again. They begged Wilfong to make more fake wolf pies.

"If I do, will you promise to go home and not come back?" Wilfong asked.

"We promise," said the head wolf.

"And use manners?" James called through the window.

"We'll try," said the head wolf.

Wilfong and the Pygg brothers made more pot pies while the wolves practiced their manners.

This time they lined up to get their pies. They tried to be polite, but they still slurped and smacked a bit. They were wolves, after all.

"May we have the recipe?" asked the head wolf, picking his teeth with a long claw.

Wilfong wrote everything down, and the head wolf put the recipe in his pocket. Then the wolves went home as they had promised, packed together in their wolfmobile.

4

Awoo, Awoo, Awooooo!

The Pygg brothers crowded around Wilfong Wolf. They patted his back and shook his paw.

"You saved us again," said Marvin.

"It was the pies that saved us," said Wilfong.

"You were the one who fooled the wolves," said Lester.

"I couldn't have done it without James's plan," said Wilfong.

"We did it together," said James. "We make a good team."

"The best," said Marvin and Lester.

They finished off the fake wolf pie for supper. Then they washed the dishes and put them away.

"Time for bed," said James.

Wilfong had to go out one door and come back in another to get to his wolf room. He dragged his feet. He wished he could be part of the Pygg family instead of living alone.

Marvin looked outside. "It's raining," he said. "You'll get wet, Wilfong. Take my umbrella."

"And my rain boots," added Lester.

"No," said James. "Sleep on our couch tonight, Wilfong. Tomorrow we'll turn your window into a door."

"Really?" said Wilfong.

"Really," said James. "You're our friend. You don't need a wolf room now. You can have your own room in our house."

Wilfong grinned with happiness. Marvin and Lester danced a jig. Then James sat down at the piano, and they all sang together in perfect harmony. *"Awoo, awoo, awooooo!"*